FOR SADIE AND THE  TOAD

OSCAR AND ARABELLA AND ORMSBY
by Neal Layton
British Library Cataloguing in Publication Data
A catalogue record of this book is available from
the British Library.
ISBN: 978 0 340 88454 6 (HB)

Copyright © Neal Layton 2007

First edition published 2007
10 9 8 7 6 5 4 3 2 1

Published by Hodder Children's Books
a division of Hachette Children's Books
338 Euston Road London NW1 3BH

Printed in China by WKT

Oscar and Arabella and ORMSBY

by Neal Layton

Hodder Children's Books

A division of Hachette Children's Books

Oscar was a WOOLLY MAMMOTH.
And so was Arabella.

They were the best of friends.

On fine sunny days they liked to go for leafy strolls through the pine forest.

Sometimes they would happen
upon secluded sunny glades.

Ormsby liked to
go for strolls
through the
pine forest too.

Oscar wasn't awfully keen on Ormsby.
Arabella thought he was quite **FUN.**

Oscar was good at balancing
and sometimes he would do
handstands to amuse Arabella.

If it started to snow Oscar would put his trunk up above Arabella to keep the snow off her a bit.

Ormsby would offer to put his arm around her to keep out the draughts.

If the storm got even worse Oscar
would suggest they get back to the
herd immediately.

Ormsby would say that Oscar was being namby-pamby and suggest they make snow sculptures.

Oscar would trumpet really **LOUDLY**.
Ormsby would trumpet really **LOUDLY**.

Oscar would stamp his **huge** feet.
Ormsby would stamp his **huge** feet.

Oscar and Ormsby
would run at
one another
and

BASH

their tusks
against one
another
and try
and

flatten
each
other.

Neither of them noticed Arabella...

Oscar and Ormsby heard her cry for help
and immediately rushed to her rescue.

Together they charged across the icy plain.

Ormsby knocked down a tree so they could cross the glacier.

Then Oscar did a handstand to help Ormsby up the ice cliff.

And after launching hundreds of **snowballs** at the enemy,

they both cartwheeled in to whisk Arabella away to safety.

That night they told the story of their heroic rescue, and though the details were somewhat confusing, everyone was glad that Arabella was safe.

None more so than Oscar, because Arabella was Oscar's very best special friend. And Oscar was Arabella's very best special friend.

And Ormsby was their friend too.

Even if they didn't get along all the time.

WOOLLY MAMMOTH
AND WOOLLY RHINOCEROS
FACTS

Woolly mammoths would have lived in herds of up to 20-50 ~~mammoths~~ mammoths of all ages. Their social lives would have been similar to the way elephants live today.

Woolly rhinoceros lived about the same time as mammoths. They would have been about 2 metres tall and weighed 2-3 tons. ⟫⟶ 2m

You might have thought Oscar and Ormsby were a bit silly showing off to Arabella.

I don't think Arabella was very impressed though...

1